CHARLIE'S HOUSE

Clyde Robert Bulla

CHARLIE'S HOUSE

Illustrated by Arthur Dorros

THOMAS Y. CROWELL   NEW YORK

Text copyright © 1983 by Clyde Robert Bulla
Illustrations copyright © 1983 by Arthur Dorros
All rights reserved. Printed in the United States of America.
No part of this book may be reproduced in any manner
whatsoever without written permission except in the case of
brief quotations embodied in critical articles and reviews.
For information address Thomas Y. Crowell, Junior Books,
10 East 53rd Street,
New York, N.Y. 10022. Published simultaneously in Canada
by Fitzhenry & Whiteside Limited, Toronto.
Designed by Harriett Barton
10 9 8 7 6 5 4 3 2 1
First Edition

Library of Congress Cataloging in Publication Data
Bulla, Clyde Robert.
    Charlie's house.

    Summary: A poor, friendless English boy, shipped to
America as an indentured servant in the early eighteenth
century, runs away from a cruel master and dreams of
building a house of his own.
    1. United States—History—Colonial period, ca.
1600-1775—Juvenile fiction. [1. United States—History
—Colonial period, ca. 1600-1775—Fiction.
2. Indentured servants—Fiction. 3. Dwellings—Fiction]
I. Dorros, Arthur, ill. II. Title.
PZ7.B912Ch 1983   [Fic]   82-45576
ISBN 0-690-04259-0
ISBN 0-690-04260-4 (lib. bdg.)

To William Lothard White

16831

Contents

CHARLIE'S HOUSE

The Way the World Is

Charlie Brig was born near the town of Durford, England, in the year 1736. He lived on a farm with his mother, father, and ten brothers and sisters. They farmed the land for Master Minton. The farm was stony and poor, and Master Minton took most of what they raised.

Charlie's House

When Charlie was eight years old he went to Durford with two of his older brothers. He had never been to town before, and there he saw something that was a great wonder to him. He saw some men building a house.

He had never thought much about houses. They were just there, like rocks or hills or trees. Now he saw how the floors and walls were made to fit together. He saw how the roof went on. After that day he looked at houses to see how they were built. He asked questions about doors and windows.

No one answered him. His brothers and sisters began to jeer when he talked about houses, and his father told him to "sing another tune." Then he knew he had said too much and made himself look foolish.

Charlie's father had never liked him. Neither had his brothers and sisters. He thought it was because of the way he looked. His hair curled and his eyes were blue. All his brothers and sisters had straight hair and gray eyes.

Sometimes he thought his mother liked him, but he was not sure. She worked from morning till night and had little time for him.

One day he wandered off to town. He wanted to see how the house looked now.

It was finished, with people living in it. He remembered it with the walls open and sky showing through the roof. He smiled as if he and the house were friends, as if they had a secret.

As he was starting home, he fell in the muddy street, and a wagon ran over him. He was pressed into the mud. Except for that, he might have been killed. As it was, he was badly hurt.

"So you had to go off to town and get yourself run over," said his father. "Now you'll be just another mouth to feed and never any use again."

Charlie could not walk. Day after day he sat in a chair and looked out the window. A little girl named Polly lived down the road, and she came to see him. She brought him things she thought were pretty—a bird's nest and bits of ribbon and small stones.

He asked her if she could find him a knife and some pieces of wood. She brought them to him.

Then he asked for reeds from the river and some of the tough, dry grass that grew by the roadside. He asked for bark from the dead oak tree across the road.

She brought everything he asked for. She watched him cut the bark and reeds and weave them together with the grass. And one day he had made a little house.

It was so neat, so pretty, with its doors and windows, its roof and tiny chimney, that she could not look at it enough. Charlie liked to look at it, too.

"I could make a better one now," he said.

"We'll have no more of that," said his father.

Because Charlie was getting well. He was able to stand again, and as soon as he could walk, he was put to work.

Before long he could walk and work as well as ever. There was no more time for play, but he thought about the little house—he had given it to Polly—and wished he might make another one.

He told his mother, "I could build a real house if I had the land to build it on."

"I could make a silk dress if I had the silk," she said, and she looked at him with tired eyes. "Listen to me. You'll never have a piece of land with your own house on it."

"Why not?" he asked.

"Because you are poor," she answered. "You were born poor, and poor you'll stay. That's the way the world is."

Master Minton

By the time Charlie was twelve, he had grown strong and tall. He was already the tallest in the family.

This did not seem to please his father. "No doubt you think yourself a man," he said. "You'll find there's more to it than standing tall and having a proud walk."

Charlie asked his mother, "Do I have a proud walk?"

"Yes, you do," she said. "You hold your head too high."

"It isn't because I am proud," said Charlie. "It's the way my head sets on my neck."

"You must learn to keep your head down," she told him.

"Why must I?" he asked.

"Because a poor boy has no right to hold up his head," she said. "You don't watch your tongue, either. Sometimes you talk when you should listen."

He tried to remember what she said. He kept his head down. He watched his tongue.

But one day he forgot.

Master Minton had come for the rent.

"I can't pay," said Charlie's father.

"So—you can't pay," said Master Minton. "How do you expect to live on my land if you can't pay?"

Master Minton

He let his eyes wander about the farm. He looked at the pigs in the sty, the chickens and geese in their pens, the horse and the cows in the pasture. "The horse looks the best of the lot," he said. "I'll have him."

Charlie's father looked down at his shoes and said nothing.

Charlie spoke. "If you take our horse, how can we plow? If we can't plow, how can we raise a crop? If we can't raise a crop, how can we *ever* pay the rent?"

Master Minton gave no sign that he had heard. "I'll have the horse," he said, "and one of the cows as well."

He drove away with the horse and cow tied to the back of his wagon.

Charlie's father turned on Charlie. He began to shout.

Charlie's mother came running. "What has he done?" she asked.

"He spoke up to Master Minton!" shouted

Charlie's father. "Master Minton was going to take the horse. Then he took the cow as well, and all because—Charlie—spoke up—to him!"

His breath was short. His face had turned red. He sat down suddenly upon the ground.

Charlie tried to help him up. His father struck at him. "Don't you put a hand on me!" he said.

"Keep away from him—go!" whispered Charlie's mother, and Charlie went off down the road.

He stayed in a field the rest of the day. When evening came, he went home. His mother was out by the gate, as if she had been waiting for him.

"You can't stay," she said. "Your brothers are looking for you. They're going to pay you back for what you did to your father."

"What did I do?" he asked.

"He's in bed—he can't move. When spoke up the way you did, it was too much for his heart. If your brothers catch you, who knows *what* they might do. Charlie, you have to go."

"Where shall I go?" he asked.

12

"*I* don't know. Just go."

"And not come back?"

"Maybe—maybe you'll find something bet-ter...." She looked away. She said, "Why did you have to do it?"

"I didn't—" he began, and she gave him a hard little push.

He went down the road. He walked quietly so that his brothers would not hear him if they were waiting in the dark.

Something Better

Charlie walked toward Durford. Except for home, it was the only place he knew.

But what was there for him in Durford? And wouldn't his brothers look for him there?

When he came to the town, he went on through its dark streets without stopping. He had a new plan. He would go to London.

The great city was a long way off—a hundred miles, he had heard people say. But once he was there, wonderful things might happen.

"Something better," his mother had said. In London there *must* be something better.

He was four days getting there. He walked more than half the way. A man in a cart gave him a ride into London, gave him half a loaf of bread and three turnips, besides.

The sun had set when they came into the city. The man let Charlie out and drove away.

Charlie looked up and down. There were people everywhere. Where had they come from? Where did they live, and how?

There were the rich, on horseback or in coaches. There were the poor in their poor clothes. Some were begging. He saw that there were many more poor than rich.

He walked about till he was tired. He found a dark doorway, and there he slept that night.

Charlie's House

In the morning he was back on the streets. By daylight he could see how dirty and ugly they were. He came to houses where food was sold. Women and men were calling, "Pies, pies—beef and pork! Get your hot pies here!"

Charlie was so hungry, the smell of food brought tears to his eyes. He thought of seizing a pie and running with it. But a boy could be hanged for less.

He went into a house where a woman was taking pies out of an oven.

"Will you give me one of those?" he asked. "I'll work for it."

"Better go wash yourself," said the woman.

A man came out of the back room.

"What's this?" he said, and he threw Charlie into the street.

Charlie almost fell. He caught hold of a lamp post and leaned against it.

A man walked past. He stopped and came back. He was fairly young, with a round, smooth

face, and he wore good clothes.

"What's the matter?" he asked. "Are you sick?"

"I—I—" Charlie looked toward the food house.

"Hungry?" asked the man.

Charlie nodded.

"Just come from the country?"

Again Charlie nodded.

"Are you alone here?"

"Yes," said Charlie.

"Where are you staying?"

"Nowhere."

"What is your name?"

"Charlie Brig."

"Mine is Fred Coker," said the man. "Come along, Charlie."

Captain Beezy

They went into another food house. This one had
tables and chairs. They sat at a table.

"I've got no money," said Charlie.

"I'll pay," said Fred.

Charlie ate two pies and washed them down
with tea. He was still hungry, but he was ashamed
to say so.

Fred asked him, "What do you think of the city?"

"Not much," answered Charlie. "It isn't the way I thought it would be."

Fred laughed. "You sound like a wise young man. Tell me, what happened to send you off to London?"

Charlie told him.

Afterward they went to Fred's home. It was two rooms in an inn near the London docks. Charlie had a wash. He put on the clean clothes Fred brought him. Then there was more to eat.

All the time, Fred seemed to be thinking.

"So you can't go home," he said.

"No," said Charlie.

"And there's not much for you in London. Boys like you come here by the hundreds. They have nowhere to turn and nothing to do. They get into trouble and they're thrown into jail. You can see that, can't you?"

"Yes," said Charlie.

"You're not like the most of them. I'd say you're a good boy, and you look strong and able to work. Charlie, did you ever hear of America?"

"Yes," said Charlie.

"Ever think of going?"

"To America? No."

"Why not?"

"It's so far."

"No place is far these days," said Fred. "You get on a ship and you go." He began telling Charlie about America. "They need people there. They need them to work on the land. You could make your fortune."

"A boy like me could go?"

"They need boys, too. Charlie, I have this friend. He's captain of a ship, and he's off to America any day now. I couldn't promise anything, but—"

"Would he take me, do you think?"

"I don't know. We could go to see him. Have you ever been on a ship?"

"No," said Charlie.

"Come along then," said Fred. "Let me do the talking. Just put yourself in my hands. And Charlie—?"

"What?"

"Can you read and write?"

Charlie shook his head.

"That doesn't matter. If there are papers to sign, I'll sign them for you. You trust me, don't you?"

"Yes," said Charlie.

The ship was in the dock, only a few steps from the inn. They went aboard, and the captain greeted them. Captain Beezy was his name. He was a short, wide man with a bald head that shone and a gold tooth that twinkled.

He took them to his cabin. They sat at a tiny table, and the men drank rum and told stories. Charlie did not understand much of the stories, but he liked hearing their voices, and he liked the smoky cabin with its dark wood walls.

After a while he heard Fred laughing and telling him to open his eyes.

Charlie sat up. He was ashamed to think he had fallen asleep.

Captain Beezy said, "Didn't you hear me, young man? You and I are shipping out together."

Charlie looked from him to Fred. Fred gave him a wink and nodded. Then Charlie knew. The captain liked him. The captain was going to take him to America!

"The adventures you'll have!" said Captain Beezy.

"A boy like you will make his fortune," said Fred.

Charlie knew he should feel excited and happy. He *was* excited, but he was a little afraid as he thought how quickly all his life was changing.

The Bond

The name of Captain Beezy's ship was *Four-and-Twenty Blackbirds*. On a fine summer morning she sailed out of London. Fred had not come to say good-bye, and Charlie was sad, since Fred was his only friend.

But the ship was crowded with young men and boys. He was sure he would make friends among them.

Some of them were loud and rough. They laughed at Charlie and called him "country."

One of the boys was a redhead named Flitters. He was near Charlie's age and size. He kept dancing about Charlie and trying to box with him.

"Leave me alone," said Charlie.

"Come on, come on," said Flitters. "Fight like a man."

On deck one day some of the others made a circle around Charlie. They pushed Flitters into the circle.

"Fight!" they said.

There was no way out of it. The two boys fought. While Flitters was dancing and boxing, Charlie knocked him down.

After that, he had an easier time of it. He and Flitters even came to be friends.

Flitters asked him, "How did you get on this ship?"

Charlie told him about Fred.

"I know who he is," said Flitters. "He works

for the captain."

"He does?"

"Yes. He gets men and boys to go to America," said Flitters, "and the captain pays him."

Charlie was puzzled. "What does he pay him for?"

"The captain gets a good price for everyone he brings to America," Flitters told him. "People in America buy our bonds from the captain."

"What are bonds?" asked Charlie.

"You don't know much, do you? Didn't Fred Coker and the captain sign a paper for you?"

Charlie tried to remember. "I think they did."

"That was your bond. Maybe Fred Coker pretended he was your father or uncle or something, and he signed you over to the captain."

Charlie was more puzzled than ever. "Signed me over—how? What does that mean?"

"It means somebody in America will buy your bond, and then you work for him. You work for seven years."

"Seven years!"

"It's not so bad," said Flitters. "Look at it this way. You'll still be young when it's over, and then the good times start. You get fifty acres of land. Anyway, that's what I get, and I should think you'd get the same. Fifty acres is enough to make a man rich. And there's more besides. You get a new suit of clothes and a shirt and shoes and stockings and a cap. Then you get two hoes and an ax. It's all there in the bond."

"But seven years! It's like—" Charlie stopped.

"Like being a slave? Is that what you mean?"

"Yes," said Charlie.

"There's a difference. We're free in seven years, but a slave goes on being a slave."

Charlie was thinking of Fred. "I thought he was my friend."

"Who? Fred Coker? Maybe he was your friend, after all. Maybe he did you a good turn without knowing it."

A New Home

In late summer *Four-and-Twenty Blackbirds* sailed
into Philadelphia harbor. The voyage to America
had taken six weeks. Charlie looked out on the
city with its rows of neat houses, both brick and
wood, and he longed to set foot on land. He had
had his fill of the sea.

Charlie's House

As soon as the ship docked, Captain Beezy lined the men and boys up on deck. "Look sharp," he said. "Here come the gentlemen."

Men had been waiting to come aboard. When the plank was down, they came running. Some pushed their way ahead of the others.

"They're going to choose," Flitters told Charlie. "Everybody wants the best."

A man chose Flitters and drew him aside.

Another man stopped in front of Charlie. "What about this one?" he asked Captain Beezy. "Can he put out a good day's work?"

"That he can," said the captain. "You'll make no mistake if you choose him. All muscle he is. And look." He caught Charlie by the chin and pulled his mouth open. "A full set of teeth."

That was how Charlie met George Chapman, the man who bought his bond. He was a quiet man with gray in his hair. He had a slow way of talking that put Charlie at ease. From the first he felt *right* with Master Chapman.

A New Home

For three days they rode together in Master Chapman's wagon. They rode through the most beautiful country Charlie had ever seen. There were woods and fields and swift little rivers. All across the land, people were going about their work. Everyone looked happy. No one looked poor.

Master Chapman talked as they rode along. Once he showed Charlie a piece of paper with writing on it. It was the bond he had bought from Captain Beezy. "Have you read this?" he asked.

"No, sir," answered Charlie.

"But you know what it means?"

"Some of it."

"You owe me seven years' work. Do you understand that?"

"Yes, sir."

"You're to give me seven years' work, unless you run away. For every time you run away, you must work two years more."

"Yes, sir," said Charlie.

"But you'll not be running away, will you?"

"I shouldn't think so, sir."

"I'll try not to give you cause," said Master Chapman, and he smiled at Charlie.

They came to the Chapman house. It was a log house set among old elm trees.

A woman came out. She looked at Charlie, and he saw the disappointment on her face.

"This is our boy," said Master Chapman. "Charlie, this is my wife, Mistress Chapman."

"I thought you were going to bring home a man," she said.

"I was slow getting on the ship, and all the men were taken," said Master Chapman. "But I'd have had to pay more for a man. Besides, I liked the look of this boy. I don't think we'll be sorry."

She came closer to the wagon. She was looking into Charlie's face.

A New Home

"No," she said, "I don't think we *will* be sorry," and she took his hand in hers.

They gave him a long, low room high under the roof. They set a place for him at the table. They gave him new clothes bought in Philadelphia.

That night he lay awake in his room and looked out the window by his bed. He saw the sheds and the road and the trees in the moonlight that was almost as bright as day. And for a little while he thought of his mother and father, his brothers and sisters. He wished they might look in on him now. He wished they might see the home that was his.

A Game of Cards

Most of the Chapman farm was covered with woods. Charlie helped clear the land, to make it ready for the plow. He and Master Chapman cut trees and pulled out stumps. The work was hard and slow, but Charlie was strong and he grew stronger.

A Game of Cards

He wondered which fifty acres would be his and where he would build his house. He thought often of his house. On a scrap of paper he had drawn a picture of it, and he carried the paper in his pocket.

When he had his own farm, he would still be near the Chapmans, he thought. He would always help them if they needed him.

Charlie came to know the neighbors. He went to barn dances with other young people. He listened to the fiddle music and watched the dancers and pretended he was dancing, too.

When the rivers and ponds froze over, he went to moonlight skating parties. But almost every night he was at home with the Chapmans. Mistress Chapman was teaching him to read and write.

A visitor came—a man named Oliver Greer. He was Master Chapman's cousin from Carolina.

He had come north on business.

He was slim and dark, with a neat, black mustache. He dressed like a gentleman, and he seemed proud of the way he looked.

He thought the Chapmans were much too good to Charlie.

"That boy thinks he's one of the family," he said.

While Master Greer was there, Charlie never ate at the table with the others.

Master Greer gave him work to do, and he never called him by name. "Boy," he would say, "shine my boots. Boy, light my pipe."

"Do as he says, Charlie," said Mistress Chapman. "It won't be for long."

But Master Greer stayed on and on. Every night he and Master Chapman sat up, drinking and playing cards.

"I do wish he would go," said Mistress Chapman. "Sometimes I'm so afraid—"

There was a change in Master Chapman. He

took to staying in his room all morning. He looked ill. He often stumbled when he walked.

Master Greer had been there almost a month when Mistress Chapman called Charlie into the kitchen. She said, "Master Greer is leaving today."

He had thought she would be glad. Instead she began to cry.

Master Chapman came in. His face was gray, and his hands shook. "Charlie, I must talk to you."

"Yes, sir," said Charlie.

"My cousin is going home," said Master Chapman, "and you—you are going with him."

Charlie heard the words, but he did not believe them. He waited.

"You are going with him," Master Chapman said again. "I lost you. I lost you in a game of cards."

"But you—" began Charlie.

Master Chapman turned away from him. "I'm sorry."

A Game of Cards

"I came to work for *you*," said Charlie. "*You* bought my bond."

"That's true, but Cousin Oliver won it from me. The bond will be the same. You'll still have your land when you've worked for it—only you'll work for him instead." Master Chapman said, "Now go. Cousin Oliver is waiting."

Charlie looked out the window. Master Greer's carriage was in front of the house. Master Greer was standing beside it.

Willow Bend

They were two weeks on the road. It was night
when Charlie first saw Willow Bend. That was
the name of Master Greer's home in Carolina.
Charlie had been asleep inside the carriage. Now
he woke and saw lights shining behind a row of
tall, white pillars.

A girl came running across the porch. She

looked no more than seven or eight. "Father!" she cried.

Master Greer jumped down from the driver's seat. He picked the little girl up in his arms. "Dessa, baby! You don't know how I've missed you!"

A man came out of the house. Master Greer spoke to him. "Take the horses."

"Yes, Master," said the man.

The girl was patting her father's pockets. "You brought me something—I know you did!"

"Yes, but not in my pocket. Come here, boy," called Master Greer.

Charlie got out of the carriage. He climbed the steps and stood on the porch.

"Who is he?" asked Dessa.

"You told me you wanted your own serving boy," said her father.

"Is he mine?" she asked.

"Yes, baby," he said.

She looked Charlie up and down. She was

frowning, with her lips pushed out.

"Don't you like him?" asked Master Greer.

"I...don't...know," she said.

"You needn't make up your mind tonight. You can look at him again tomorrow." Master Greer picked her up and carried her into the house.

Charlie stood there. He did not know where to go or what to do. After a while a woman came out. She was old and black, and she had a purple cloth tied about her head.

"Come along," she said.

He followed her inside and up a stairway. She showed him a small, bare bedroom.

"You can sleep there." She gave him a lighted candle and went away.

Charlie blew out the candle and lay down. The smell of flowers came through the window. It was heavy and sweet. He breathed it and felt sick.

In the morning the woman woke him and led him out back. Behind the big house were rows of little houses. One was a bathhouse. She left him there with two young black men.

They washed Charlie's hair. They gave him a bath in a tub of hot water.

Afterward they had clean clothes ready for him to put on. The clothes were some that he had brought from Master Chapman's.

The woman came again and led him into the big house.

"You go in there," she said.

He went into a sunny room where Master Greer and Dessa were having breakfast.

The little girl clapped her hands. "I like him better now," she cried. "I like him *ever* so much better!"

"I hoped you would," said her father.

"I like the way his hair shines." Dessa got up from her chair to look at Charlie. "But his clothes are ugly. I'll have to have something made for him. I'll need a name for him, too."

"He has a name," said her father.

"Has he? What is it? *You* tell me," she said to Charlie. "Speak. What is your name?"

"Charlie Brig," he told her.

"Charlie Brig—Charlie Brig. That's funny." She did a little dance, hopping from one foot to the other. "Oh, it's going to be such fun having someone all my own!"

The Tea Party

Dessa had clothes made for Charlie—a jacket and short breeches. They were of green silk. She found white stockings for him, and black slippers with silver buckles.

He put on his new clothes. She made him walk up and down for her. She called the other servants to look.

"Isn't he beautiful!" she said. "Now he needs

something to wear on Sunday—a white suit, maybe. But isn't he beautiful in the green!"

Charlie was Dessa's own servant. When she went riding, he helped her up on her pony. When she had her meals, he stood behind her chair. Sometimes he carried her dolls from one room to another.

He saw the other servants laughing at him.

Dessa gave a tea party for her dolls. She had a little tea set, with real tea in the pot.

"Pour the tea, Charlie," she said, and he filled the cups.

She took a sip of her tea and made a face. "This is *cold*!" She picked up her riding whip and gave him a cut across the legs with it.

He jumped and dropped the teapot. It broke on the floor.

"You broke it. My best teapot, and you broke it!" She began to scream.

Her father came into the room. "Baby, what *is* it?"

"See what he did." She was kicking Charlie and striking at him with her whip.

"I thought you wanted him," said her father. "I thought you liked him."

"Well, I don't," she said. "I hate him!"

Again Charlie's life had changed. He was no longer a house servant. He was a field hand.

He lived in one of the tiny houses behind the big house. He hoed in the tobacco fields with the other workers. Most of them were men, but some were women and children, and all were black.

He asked a girl, "Are you a slave?"

She looked frightened, and all she said was, "I don't know."

At first the others left Charlie to himself, but after a few days they seemed to grow used to him. One of the boys began to talk with him as they worked side by side. The boy's name was Norrie. He had bright, black eyes, and he could talk

without moving his mouth.

"I know who you are," he said, "and I know why they put you in the field. My mama works in the big house, and she told me."

"I'd rather be here," said Charlie.

"You don't say!" said Norrie.

"In the field I know what I'm supposed to do. I don't want to go back to the big house."

But field work was hard. The rows were long. The sun beat down on the workers' heads and backs.

Charlie said one day, "I wish I had a drink of water."

"So do I," said Norrie, "but we have to wait till they tell us."

"I'm not going to wait," said Charlie. "When I get to the end of this row I'm going to get myself a drink."

"Where?" asked Norrie.

"Out of the river."

"You don't dare," said Norrie.

"You'll see," said Charlie.

At the end of the row, he slipped under the fence. The river was there, at the edge of the field. He slid down the bank, put his face into the water, and drank. Then he slipped back into the field. He was gone hardly a minute.

Norrie looked scared. "You'll catch it now," he said.

"Are you going to tell?" asked Charlie.

"No, but somebody will," said Norrie, "and you'll wish you'd never been born."

"Why?" asked Charlie.

"When Master comes home, you'll find out."

"Where is Master?" asked Charlie.

"He and Miss Dessa, they went to the city. They went to find a boy to take your place."

———

That evening Charlie was sitting in front of his small house.

Norrie came by. "They just got home," he said.

"Master and Miss Dessa."

"Did they find another boy?" aked Charlie.

"They looked," said Norrie, "but they couldn't find one to please Miss Dessa. Charlie—"

"What?"

"Master found out about your drink of water."

"Did you tell him?"

"No, but somebody did." Norrie shook his head. "I wouldn't want to be you."

"Thank You, Miss Dessa"

Early in the morning there was a meeting in front of the big house. All the field workers and house servants were there.

Master Greer came down the steps. His eyes found Charlie. "You," he said. "Come here."

Charlie stepped forward.

"*Thank You, Miss Dessa*"

"You left your work yesterday," said Master Greer.

"Not for long, sir." Charlie's throat had gone dry. "I wanted a drink—"

"You left your work!" Master Greer spoke to one of the field workers. "Get him ready."

The man pulled off Charlie's shirt and tied him to a tree.

Master Greer made a speech. "I hope you will all learn something today. This boy has had an easy life. He thinks he can do as he pleases here. Yesterday he broke the rules. This is what happens when you break the rules."

The front door opened. Dessa ran down the steps.

"What are you doing?" she asked.

"Go back inside," said her father.

"Are you going to whip Charlie?"

"This is not for you to see," said Master Greer. "Go back inside."

"I won't! You can't whip Charlie. I won't let you."

"But baby," said her father, "he has to be punished."

"Not unless I say so. He's mine."

"Not any longer. You said you didn't want him."

"I never said it."

"Baby, you *did*."

"If I did, I changed my mind. Let him go."

"I can't—" He stopped as she began to scream. He tried to pick her up in his arms. She beat at him with her fists.

Charlie heard him say something in a low voice. One of the field hands came over to the tree. He untied Charlie and let him go.

Charlie was back in the big house. He was there with Dessa in the sunroom, among the potted plants. She was sitting on the window seat. She was smiling now.

"Aren't you glad I took you back?" she asked.

"Well, aren't you?...Speak up, Charlie."

"Yes, Miss Dessa," he said.

"Because if I hadn't, you know what would have happened to you."

"Yes, Miss Dessa."

"So you'd better be good. If you're not, I'll give you back to my father." She got up off the window seat. "Come here."

He went to her.

"Kneel down," she said.

He knelt before her.

"Kiss my hand."

He kissed her hand.

"Say, 'Thank you, Miss Dessa.'"

"Thank you, Miss Dessa."

"Say, 'Thank you, Miss Dessa, for saving me.'"

"Thank you, Miss Dessa, for saving me."

"Now you can go to the stable and clean my pony's stall. I don't want you in the house anymore today. Not in those dirty clothes. Have a bath and be sure to wash your hair. In the morning you come in and put on your suit and— Charlie!"

"Yes, Miss Dessa."

Her eyes had grown narrow. "Was that an ugly look I saw on your face?"

"No, Miss Dessa."

"I won't stand for any ugly looks. You'd better remember that. And from now on, you belong to me. You'd better remember that, too."

"Yes, Miss Dessa," he said.

Three Men

Charlie sat on his bed that night. He had opened the door, and coolness came into the little house. It was his last night at Master Greer's. That much he knew. His thoughts had taken him no further.

He had asked himself where he could go. He had thought of Master and Mistress Chapman's. Would they make a place for him, or would they give him back to Master Greer?

He knew the answer. They had given him to Master Greer once, and they would again.

In the Chapman woods there were hiding places. But how could he find his way there? He never could.

Someone came to the doorway and looked in.

"You there?"

It was Norrie.

"Yes," answered Charlie.

Norrie sat down in the doorway. "You going to the big house tomorrow?"

Charlie said nothing.

"My mama says you're going back to the big house. Everybody says so."

"Leave me alone," said Charlie.

"They take you out of the fields and put you back in the big house. You don't like that?"

Three Men

"Just leave me alone," said Charlie.

Norrie was still for a while. Then he slid a little way into the house. "I saw you at supper," he whispered. "I saw you put the bread in your pocket. Why did you put the bread in your pocket?"

Charlie did not answer.

"You better not do it," said Norrie.

"Do what?"

"What you been thinking about."

"How do you know what I've been thinking?"

"I know. If you run away—"

"I never said I was running away."

"You don't have to *say* it. You listen to me. If you do run away, you don't want to go north."

"Why not?"

"Because they'll catch you. And you don't want to go south or west. They got traps there, too. Charlie—"

"What?"

"The best way to go is east. If you think you

have to go, go east to Black Swamp. Nobody can find you there."

———

Norrie had gone. Charlie had been waiting. Now the big house was dark and quiet, and he left the little house and closed the door softly.

He went to the stables. He knew Cato, the groom who slept there at night. He called his name.

A sleepy voice answered. "Who is it?"

"It's Charlie."

"Who?"

"Charlie. You know me, Cato. I used to come for Miss Dessa's pony. I'm back in the big house now."

"I know. What you want?"

"Master sent me to fetch the black mare."

"This time of night?"

Charlie had the answer ready. "Master's going night fishing."

Three Men

Cato made grumbling sounds, but he lighted a lantern and put a saddle and bridle on the black mare. He was beginning to look doubtful.

"Are you sure—?" he began.

"I'll take her," said Charlie.

He led the mare past the big house and into the road. He turned her head to the east. Almost before he was in the saddle, she was off.

He had seen people ride. A few times he had ridden an old mule in from the fields. That was all he knew about riding. He held to the saddle, and the mare took him along.

He could see the road a little way ahead, and he could see a patch of stars low in the sky. He watched the stars.

After a while the mare slowed to a trot, then to a walk. Just before sunrise, he turned off the road and tied her in a thicket. He lay down under a tree to rest and eat a piece of bread he had carried in his pocket.

He thought how far he had come, and he

wished he might keep on riding. But the word must be out already—"Watch for a runaway boy on a black mare." Better if he turned her loose and went ahead on foot.

He lay back and looked at the sky. It seemed to swim before his eyes. He was tired, and he could feel himself dropping off to sleep.

He woke with the sun in his eyes. Three men stood before him. He knew who they were. They had often come to the big house to go hunting with Master Greer.

One of them said, "This boy runs away in style."

"Yes," said another. "On Master Greer's mare."

They were laughing. They sounded almost friendly. But when Charlie looked at their faces, he was afraid.

The Whip

They played a game with him. They were giving him a chance to go free, they said. They told him to run, and he ran.

One of the men had a long, leather whip. When he snapped it, it reached out like a snake and caught Charlie about the legs. When the man jerked the whip, Charlie fell.

The Whip

They played the game again and again. Each time Charlie ran a little more slowly. At last he fell and lay still.

"Run!" the men said, and Charlie felt the whip sting his shoulder, but he did not move.

He heard the men talking.

"Shall we take him in now?"

"No hurry. He won't be going anywhere for a while."

"Is Oliver coming this way?"

"He said he might. We'd better wait."

"Why don't we get the guns? Maybe another flock will come, and then—"

The voices moved away. Charlie heard the sound of guns. The men were firing at something. At birds flying over?

Charlie lifted his head. There were bushes in front of him. He began to crawl toward them.

He reached the bushes. He was hidden by them. He bent low and tried to run, but he was slow. In another moment he would be missed.

The men would be after him, and he could not outrun them.

He looked for a place to hide.

Just ahead was a stream with a tangle of roots along its bank. He slid down into the water. It was not deep.

He crouched in the shadow of the bank. He pulled some floating sticks and leaves over his face. He bent backward until only his nose and mouth were above the water. He could breathe through the sticks and leaves.

Once the bank shook, as if someone were running almost above his head.

Then all was quiet.

He tried to be as still as a rock or the trunk of a tree. He began to feel cramped and cold, and he moved his arms and legs a little. Slowly he lifted his head. He saw no one, yet for all he knew, the men might be near.

Not until night did he climb out of the stream. All the time he was watching, listening.

The Whip

From now on, he would make no mistakes. He would be swift as a deer and cunning as a fox, and he would never be caught again.

The River

By night he followed the roads, except where they led past houses. Houses meant people and barking dogs.

By day he disappeared into the woods and became part of their stillness and shadows. He found water there when he was thirsty. He found berries and bitter acorns to eat.

The River

Once he heard voices, and he hid in the berry bushes just before men came walking by.

Another time he thought he was caught. It was in the daylight. He had come out of hiding to look for food, and he came face to face with a man leading a cow.

The man stared at him. Charlie stared back. Neither spoke, and the man went on.

Charlie ran from the place. He walked through a stream to hide his trail.

When he took to the roads again, he started at every strange sound. He had been seen. How long would it be before Master Greer and the hunters closed in about him?

He lost count of the days and nights. Sometimes he was ready to believe Black Swamp was only a dream.

Then it was there before him. He had been sleeping in a thicket on a hilltop. When he looked out in the noon brightness, he saw the dark woods ahead. They stretched as far as he

could see. A mist hung over them like a long, low cloud.

Black Swamp, he thought. It *must* be Black Swamp.

Without waiting for night, he started toward it. He would need light for finding his way.

He saw no farms or roads near the swamp. He found himself in a sea of tall grass. While he was fighting his way through it, night fell, and he lay down to sleep.

In the morning he came out into a clearing. A shed was there, the kind a hunter or fisherman might use. The front was open, and he could see into it. No one was there.

A path led from the shed to a river. On the bank was a boat with a pole beside it.

Charlie saw no one, heard no one. He went quickly down the path and pushed the boat into the water. He held it there while he picked up the pole. He stepped into the boat and poled himself out into the river.

There was a current that tugged at the boat, dragging it toward the swamp.

He put the pole down, leaned over the side, and drank. The water was brown. It had an odd, sharp taste.

Now he was among trees that shut out the sunlight. The boat began to tip to one side. It was taking on water. It was sinking.

He poled it out of the current. There were vines overhead, and he caught hold of one and swung himself to shore. He rested on the roots of a tree before he tried to go any farther.

Time after time he fell, and the soft earth pulled him down. Each time he dragged himself out he felt weaker.

He was ill. It was the water, he thought. He had drunk too much.

There was night, then day, then night again.

The River

He dreamed of faces looking down through leaves and branches. In the dream a voice was speaking strange words, and the voice sounded like his own. Once a great, white flower seemed to burst open before his eyes.

He thought he was being carried. He thought he was rocking in a boat. He heard someone laughing—or was it the cry of a bird?

Drogo

He lay in a nest of leaves. Overhead he saw the sky, deep blue, with a few white clouds. There was woodsmoke in the air.

He tried to sit up, and a man bent over him. The man's hair was white, his skin was dark. His face was bright and gentle and smiling.

Drogo

"Lie back," he said. "You are still weak." He asked, "Do you know me now?"

"No," said Charlie, yet it seemed the face was one he *should* know.

"I am Drogo," said the man. "I found you, remember? I saw the big bird over the swamp. He was following you, and I followed him until I found you. It was good for you that I did."

"Where are we?" asked Charlie.

"This is our island."

From where he lay, Charlie could see woods and a few huts. He thought he saw a man among the trees, and he cried out.

"Do not fear," said Drogo. "You are safe. Master Greer will not find you here."

Charlie felt a chill when he heard the name. "Do you know him?"

"Only from what you said. You talked to me. All the days you were ill, you talked. You do not remember?"

"No."

"Your story is much like mine. I, too, ran away. I was lost, and I found this island in the swamp. I was the first ever to find it, I think. Now it is home for me and for others."

"What others?"

"Others who ran away. I helped them. I brought them here."

Charlie met the others. There were nine men, five women, a boy, and a girl. Some of them talked with him. Some kept away, almost as if they were afraid of him.

He learned their names. He saw how they hunted, fished, and tended their gardens. They had hoes, knives, and axes.

"Where did you get these?" he asked.

"I brought them from outside," answered Drogo. "I can go back and forth without being seen. There are ways I know."

Drogo

Charlie lived in Drogo's hut. As he grew stronger, he found work to do. He made fish-hooks out of bones. He wove a hammock of reeds and grasses.

The day came when he said to Drogo, "I am well now."

They were sitting on the floor of the hut, mending a fishnet. Drogo stopped working and gave Charlie a long look. "So. You are well."

"Yes. I am well enough to go."

"Where?"

"Outside. Into the world."

"You have good hands, and a good head, I think. We are glad of your help. Why not stay?"

"*Live* here, you mean?"

"Do you know a better hiding place?"

"No, but..." Charlie said slowly, "I don't always want to be hiding."

"You want to go where Master Greer will find you and take you back?"

"No, but in all this land there must be places

where I can go—where Master Greer could never find me."

"You are not happy here?"

"Sometimes, but sometimes I feel the swamp around me like a prison!"

"Ah, yes..." Drogo looked away. His eyes had grown sad.

"Don't *you* ever think of going away and finding a place out in the world?" asked Charlie.

"You forget."

"What?"

"The color of my skin. Whoever saw me would know what I am—a slave who ran away. But if this is a prison to you, then you must go."

"Will you help me?" asked Charlie.

"Yes, when it is time."

"Tomorrow?"

"You are young, Charlie. As you grow older, you will change. You may change so much that Master Greer would not know you on the road. Then you will be safe out in the world."

"That would take years!"

"Perhaps not so many. Think on it. Sleep tonight and think again—and tell me what you are thinking."

—————

That night Charlie slept and woke and slept again. He was awake at daylight. He went outside and stood there, looking.

Near the hut was a little hill. He walked slowly around it, seeing it from every side. He climbed to the top of it.

A breeze blew in from across the swamp, and branches moved over his head. The sky was red where the sun would soon be rising.

Drogo had come outside.

"This may be the place," said Charlie.

"The place?"

"To build my house," said Charlie.

Drogo did not seem to understand, and Charlie told him, "If I stay, I'll need a house."

Then Drogo began to smile. "Ah," he said. "Ah, yes."

The house was there in Charlie's mind, with walls of small logs and a roof of leaves and grass. It was straight and strong, but a little rough, because he had only an ax for smoothing the wood. His next house would be better.

ABOUT THE AUTHOR

Clyde Robert Bulla is one of America's best-known writers for young people. The broad scope of his interests has led him to write more than fifty distinguished books on a variety of subjects, including travel, history, science, and music. He has received a number of awards for his contributions to the field of children's books, including, for SHOESHINE GIRL, awards in three states—Oklahoma, Arkansas, and South Carolina—that were voted on by school children.

Clyde Bulla's early years were spent on a farm near King City, Missouri. He now lives and works in the bustling city of Los Angeles. When he is not busy writing a book, he loves to travel.

ABOUT THE ARTIST

Arthur Dorros was born in Washington, D.C. He was graduated with honors from the University of Wisconsin. He has traveled through most of the fifty states as well as throughout Japan, Indonesia, Thailand, Nepal, and South America. He is the author and illustrator of two picture books, PRETZLES and ALLIGATOR SHOES.